Belle & Boo
and the
Goodnight Kiss

Mandy Sutcliffe

ORCHARD

To my wonderful friend Kate, for her inspiration, determination and organisation

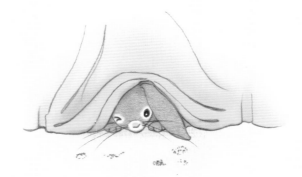

ORCHARD BOOKS
338 Euston Road, London NW1 3BH
Orchard Books Australia
Level 17/207 Kent Street, Sydney, NSW 2000

First published in 2012 by Orchard Books
First published in paperback in 2013

ISBN 978 1 40831 611 5

Text by Gillian Shields
Text © Orchard Books 2012
Illustrations © Mandy Sutcliffe 2012

The right of Mandy Sutcliffe to be identified as the illustrator of this work
has been asserted by her in accordance with the Copyright, Designs and Patents Act, 1988.

With thanks to Mark Burgess

A CIP catalogue record for this book is available from the British Library.

1 3 5 7 9 10 8 6 4 2

Printed in China

Orchard Books is a division of Hachette Children's Books,
an Hachette UK company.
www.hachette.co.uk

This is **Belle**, and this is **Boo**.

They are always together –
on sunny days,
rainy days,
and dreamy let's-be-lazy days.

"It's been a busy day," said Belle.
"Very lots of busy," agreed Boo.

"And I'm a nice kind of sleepy,"
said Belle.
"Very sleepy," yawned Boo.

The birds and squirrels were all going to bed.

Even the sun was getting ready for bed.

"Is it our **bedtime**, too?" asked Boo.

"Almost," said Belle. "But it's **bath time** first."

Belle had a warm, splashy bath, with two little boats
bobbing on the water.

Boo wasn't sure about baths.
He blew bubbles instead.

"Is it **bedtime** now?" he asked.

"Almost," said Belle. "First we have to
brush Raggedy Doll's hair."

"And we have to tuck up Snuffly Elephant
and Honey Bear in their basket," said Belle.

"It's a very cosy sort of basket," said Boo.

"Now is it time for bed?" asked Boo.
"Almost," said Belle. "After our milk and cookies."

Boo was *very* sure about milk and cookies.
"I can't go to sleep without milk
and cookies," he said happily.

"Now we have to clean our teeth!" said Belle.

"And we mustn't forget our **bedtime** story,"
Boo said, getting out his favourite book.

It was an **exciting** story about a princess and a dragon.
Belle read the words and Boo looked at the pictures.

Then he decided to be a noisy,

chasing-up-and-down dragon.

"Boo!" laughed Belle. "It's supposed to be bedtime!"

But Boo wasn't quite ready for bed.

"Being a dragon has made me thirsty," he said,

in a hot kind of voice.

Belle smiled and went to fetch a glass of water.

"I know," said Boo. "I'll hide!

That will be a **Big Surprise** for Belle.

She likes **surprises**."

Boo tried hiding in Honey Bear and Snuffly Elephant's
basket, but it was a bit full.

He tried hiding under the bed,
but it was a bit dusty.

"Atishoo!" said Boo.

He tried hiding in the toy fort, with its tall walls
and pull-up bridge. But he wasn't very comfortable.

And then he found the perfect place . . .

When Belle came back, Boo had vanished.

He wasn't in the basket . . .

. . . or under the bed . . .

. . . or waiting behind the door to

jump out as a Big Surprise.

"Oh, no," said Belle. "I can't find Boo!

And I haven't given him his

goodnight kiss!"

Boo had forgotten about the most important part of bedtime!

"I'm here!" Boo called, jumping out

from under the covers.

"I'm here!

I want my kiss!"

"Oh, Boo," said Belle,

"I looked everywhere for you!

I'm so happy to see you."

"I'm glad it's **bedtime** now," yawned Boo, as they
snuggled into bed. "Will tomorrow be a busy day?"
"Very lots of busy," smiled Belle.

"And will we be together?" asked Boo.
"Always," said Belle.

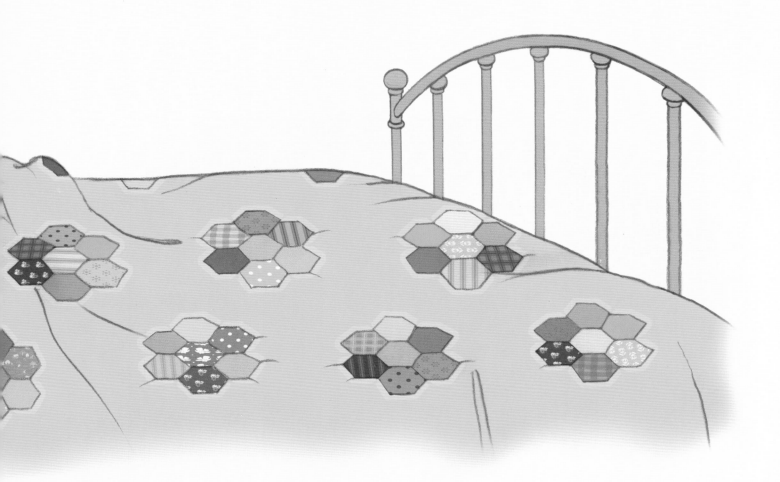

Then she gave Boo the **biggest**,
best goodnight kiss ever . . .

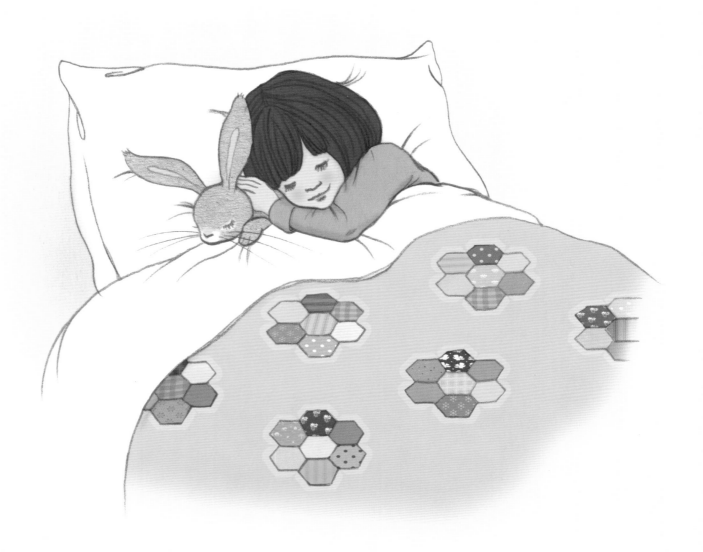

. . . and Belle and Boo fell fast asleep together.